THE RINGDOVES

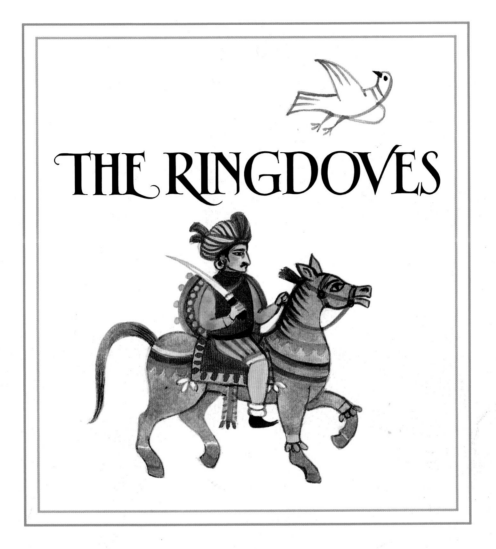

From THE FABLES OF BIDPAI

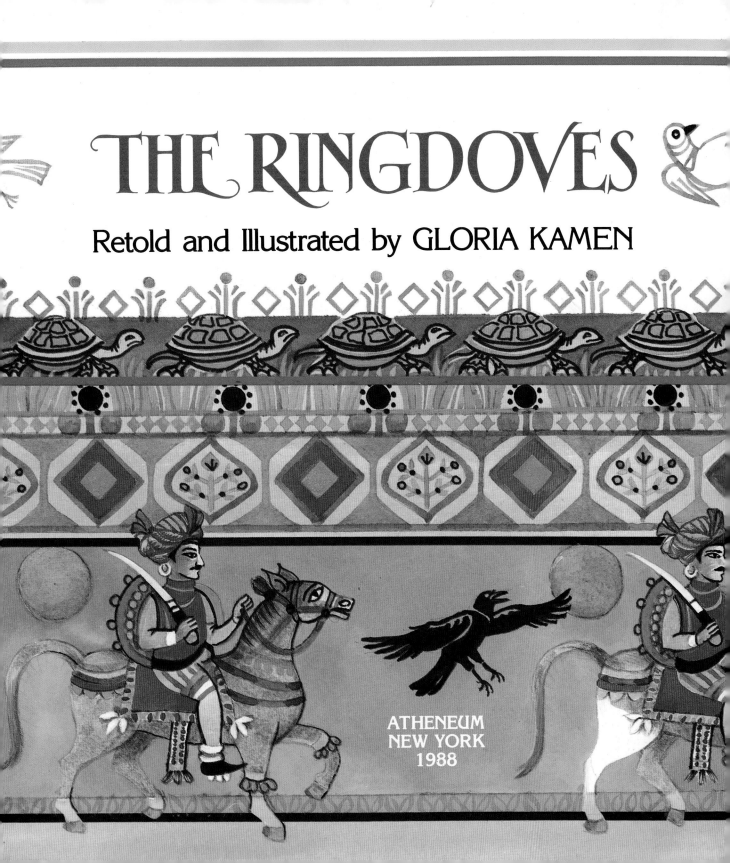

THE RINGDOVES

Retold and Illustrated by GLORIA KAMEN

ATHENEUM
NEW YORK
1988

To All My Readers

JUN 1 '88

Atheneum
Macmillan Publishing Company
866 Third Avenue, New York, NY 10022
Collier Macmillan Canada, Inc.

Type set by Fisher Composition, New York City
Printed and bound by Toppan Printing Company, Inc., Japan
Book design by Gloria Kamen
Lettering on the half title and title page by Anita Karl
First Edition

10 9 8 7 6 5 4 3 2 1

Library of Congress Cataloging-in-Publication Data

Kamen, Gloria.   The ringdoves.

An adaptation from the Fables of Bidpai.
SUMMARY: In this Indian fable about loyalty and
friendship, several animals band together
to elude the hunter.
   [1. Fables.   2. Folklore—India] I. Fables of
Bidpai. English. Selections.   II. Title.
PZ8.2.K36Ri   1988   398.2'452'0934   [E]   87-17404
ISBN 0-689-31312-8

A TALE ABOUT FRIENDSHIP

Long, long ago in India there lived a king and his trusted advisor, Bidpai. The king, unhappy over the many stories he had heard about deceit and envy, asked Bidpai to tell him a tale about true friendship. "How can there be love and loyalty," asked the king, "even between strangers?"

"Ah, sire," answered the advisor, "in times of danger the loyalty of one's friends is a richness beyond measure." With these words Bidpai began his story of the ringdoves.

In a mighty forest, where many hunters and fowlers came to hunt, stood a large and splendid tree. In its branches, rich in fruit and foliage, lived a wise crow. One day as he was flying toward the city in search of food, the crow saw a hunter spread his net below the tree, covering it with ripe safflower seeds. A flock of ringdoves flew by and, not noticing the net, began to feast on the seeds. The snare pulled tightly and the doves were trapped in the net.

When the hunter saw the captured doves, he was overjoyed and started toward the tree. The king of the doves called out to his followers not to be afraid. "Let us unite and fly away together before the hunter reaches us," he said. The birds flapped their wings in unison and took off with the net still wrapped around them just as the hunter approached.

The angry hunter followed below while the crow, curious to know what would happen next, flew after them. The doves flew over hills and houses, eluding the unhappy hunter, and landed near the burrow of their friend Zirak, the mouse.

"Ho! Friend Zirak," called the king of the doves, "please come quickly!"

Zirak recognized his friend's voice and came out of his hole. Seeing the birds trapped in the net, he knew what he must do and began to gnaw at the ropes until they were cut through. The doves, delighted to be free again, thanked the mouse before flying off. Zirak returned to his burrow.

Impressed by what he had seen, the crow decided to stay. He called to Zirak, the mouse, and told him he would like to be his friend. The mouse was not at all sure he could trust the large crow, for crows are known to be the natural enemies of mice. Zirak would not leave the safety of his house and he asked the crow to leave.

"But mouse," said the crow, "until today we have never met. How can you call me your enemy?"

Finally convinced that the crow meant him no harm, the mouse came out of his burrow and accepted the offer of friendship. Through time their friendship grew and they came to rely on one another. The crow would bring delicacies for the mouse, and the mouse saved grains of rice he found in his wanderings for the crow.

One day the crow noticed that the town was growing closer and closer to their woods and suggested that they find a safer place to live. "Further south is a pond where my friend the tortoise lives," he told the mouse. "The woods nearby are filled with seeds and nuts of all kinds." The mouse agreed to go, and the crow, holding onto the mouse by his tail, flew to the pond of the tortoise. The tortoise was so astonished to see the crow and mouse flying together that he plunged headlong into the water.

"Do not be afraid!" said the crow. "The mouse and I are friends. We have come to live on the banks of your pond in peace and friendship."

The tortoise came out of the water to welcome them and the crow began to build his nest in a tree while the mouse dug a burrow at its roots.

The crow, the mouse, and the tortoise enjoyed each others' company and passed their days in comfort and harmony. One day, a gazelle rushed to the pond as though pursued by hunters. Frightened, the tortoise jumped into the pond, the mouse ran to his burrow, and the crow flapped his wings and hid in the branches of a tree.

When they saw that no hunters were approaching and that the animal appeared only to be thirsty, they came out of hiding. The gazelle told them that he had indeed run away from hunters. The three friends then agreed to ask the gazelle to join them in their peaceful place and to share with them their ample food and drink.

The gazelle remained at the pond and it became the custom of the four friends to meet each day to take their meals together.

One day the gazelle failed to appear, which greatly worried the others. They feared that some misfortune had befallen him and suggested that the crow fly off in search of the gazelle.

The crow took to the air and soon discovered the unhappy gazelle caught in a trap. After assuring the gazelle that he would return quickly, the crow flew back to tell the mouse and the tortoise what he had seen. The three then set out to rescue their friend.

When they reached the gazelle, the mouse began to chew at the ropes. The crow and the tortoise worried, meanwhile, about what they should do if the hunter returned. There was no time to lose, for though the gazelle, now freed of the trap, could run quickly, the mouse could hide, and the crow fly, the tortoise was too slow to escape. As they talked, the crow spied the hunter returning for his catch.

The gazelle and mouse ran off. The crow hid in a tree, but the poor tortoise could not get away. The hunter seized the tortoise and bound him with a sturdy rope. He slung him over his shoulder and started to walk toward his village.

Out of sight of the hunter, the friends gathered to think of a plan to rescue their captured friend. The crow asked the gazelle to lie down in the path of the hunter and pretend to be wounded. At the same time, he, the crow, would hover over him as though picking at a wound, hoping in this way to deceive the approaching hunter.

There was no time to lose, for the hunter could be heard approaching the bend in the path. Following the crow's advice, the gazelle lay on his side with the crow perched over him. The mouse, meanwhile, hid in the underbrush nearby.

When the hunter arrived and saw what he believed was a wounded gazelle, he dropped the tortoise and went after the larger animal. Before he could reach him, the gazelle jumped up and ran into the dense underbrush, luring the hunter deep into the forest. The mouse then ran to the tortoise and gnawed at the ropes. By the time the tired hunter returned, the four friends were safely out of sight.

The man, ashamed and disappointed at having been fooled, returned to his village with nothing to show for his hunt again. The ringdoves had flown away with his net, the gazelle had broken out of his trap and even the slow tortoise had somehow managed to escape. From that day forward the unhappy hunter decided he would do his hunting in another part of the forest.

The crow, the mouse, the tortoise, and the gazelle settled once more beside the pond in the forest where they lived together in peace and happiness for the rest of their days.

The End

About the Ringdoves and the Fables of Bidpai

The original fables of Bidpai were written in India around the year 300 B.C. by a Brahmin sage believed to be named Bidpai. A forerunner of Aesop's Fables, these tales were designed to teach moral precepts, to instruct princes on how to rule, and to illustrate the conflicts between good and evil. The animals in the stories are given human traits and ambitions, such as greed, cruelty, envy, treachery, kindness, and loyalty.

News of this wonderful set of stories reached the court of one of the kings of Persia, who sent his physician to India to obtain a copy of the ancient manuscript. It was then translated by the physician into the Persian tongue, Pahlavi.

In about 750 A.D., the tales, now called "Kalila and Dimna" after the two jackals in the first story, were translated to Arabic and spread throughout the Near East. Children and adults alike have been delighted and instructed by these fables for centuries.

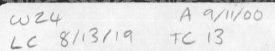